P9-DMA-432

P9-DMA-432

In memory of my entire family who perished during the Holocaust, to my late husband Fred and to my current family: Miriam, Joel, Ari, Leora, Joel, Barbara, Michal and Ben.

Turner Publishing Company
424 Church Street • Suite 2240 • Nashville, Tennessee 37219
445 Park Avenue • 9th Floor • New York, New York 10022

www.turnerpublishing.com

Leopold

This is a work of fiction. All the characters and events portrayed in this book are either products of the author's imagination or are used fictitiously.

Illustrator: Suzanne Beaky
Cover design: Maddie Cothren
Book design: Maddie Cothren

Library of Congress Cataloging-in-Publication Data on file
ISBN: 978-1-63026-918-0
Printed in the United States of America
15 16 17 18 19 0 9 8 7 6 5 4 3 2

"One who strengthens his or her self image is called a person of courage."
Commentary on the Song of Songs, Ch. 4

LEOPOLD

DR. RUTH WESTHEIMER AND PIERRE LEHU
ILLUSTRATED BY SUZANNE BEAKY

TURNER
PUBLISHING COMPANY

Grandma Ruth went to answer the door
to find Ben, her grandson, looking down at the floor.

She led him in and asked, "Why are you so sad?"
"A good boy like you wouldn't do something bad."

"Grandma it's not what I did that makes me frown,
but what I have to do that's got me so down."

"Tell your grandma what's spoiling your day,
and maybe I can make it go away."

"Last week Mom signed me up for a soccer team.
It made me so mad that I wanted to scream!
I complained, but she refused to listen to me,
and now the first practice is today at three!"

"What's wrong with soccer?" asked Grandma Ruth.
"It seems like fun to tell you the truth.
Plus, all of that running is good for you,
so instead of *one* reason to play, there's two!"

"That's what Mom said, but she doesn't know,
I'm no good at sports, which is why I'm so low.
I'll go out on that field and miss every kick,
and that's why my stomach is feeling so sick."

"Ben, you've got a problem without a doubt,
but I know a story that might help you out.
So listen to this tale about a young turtle,
who also faced a problem he couldn't hurdle."

All the young turtles were sunning on rocks.
There was Boxy, Snappy, Shelly, and Socks.
They were busy soaking up the sun's rays.
Something they did on beautiful days.

Only Leopold remained on the shore.
It's not that he liked the shade so much more,
but he was too afraid to leave his safe home,
and so he stayed in one place, never to roam.

The other turtles thought Leo liked being alone,
but in fact he felt very sad all on his own.

He really wanted to be on a rock in the sun,
and being alone was certainly no fun.

But each time Leo tried to stick his neck out,
his stomach grew tight and his heart filled with doubt.

Inside his shell he knew there was safety.
Outside lay dangers that frightened him greatly.

It seemed like his shell came with a lock
that kept him inside, but then came a knock.

Leopold wondered who it could be,
but he was too scared to look out and see.

"Hey Leo, it's me, Freddy the frog.
How come you're acting like a bump on a log?
You never ever come out of your shell,
even though everything out here is swell!"

"Freddy, how do I know it's safe outside?
I wish I could leave, but I can't decide."

"Leo, if you stay in your shell, safe you'll be,
but then you can never truly be free."

Leopold thought about what he had heard
and decided to take the frog at his word.

He popped out his head from inside his shell,
and then his four feet came out as well.

"Inside my shell I felt so secure,
but it's nice out here, that's for sure."
"Hey Leo," called Boxy from out on the water.

So Leopold slowly made his way to the shore,
and soon, in the water, he began to explore.
He climbed up on a rock and into the sun.
Never before had he had so much fun.

"Now I realize the mistake that I made.
Staying in my shell had me stuck in the shade.
It's true taking a risk was a little scary,
but outside my shell I feel so merry!"

"So, Ben, is in your shell where you want to stay?
Doing the same thing day after day?"

"You know, I see your point Grandma Ruth.
It seems Leopold the Turtle showed me the truth."

"If the turtle can take a risk, so can I.
From now on I must try not to be so shy.

I can kick a ball. It's not so hard.
In fact, I've been practicing in our yard."

Grandma Ruth looked at her watch and said,
"It's almost three, now you go ahead."

And so Ben scooted off toward the field,
a little afraid but with a new shield.

Later that day Grandma Ruth's door opened wide,
and her grandson Ben came running inside.

"You were right, Grandma. It was out of control.
Believe it or not, I scored a goal!"

"That's terrific, Ben. You make me feel proud.
At your first game, I'll be part of the crowd."

"You can cheer our team to the winner's circle.
We picked a great name. We're called the Turtles!"

ABOUT THE AUTHORS

DR. RUTH K. WESTHEIMER is known by most children as "Dr. Ruth Wordheimer" on PBS KIDS' *Between the Lions*. She is a therapist and an expert on many family issues. Dr. Westheimer is the author of 39 books including *Grandma on Wheels*. She is a devoted grandparent of four.

PIERRE LEHU has worked in public relations for forty years. He is a literary agent, publicist, and has written twenty-five books. Pierre is also a devoted grandparent.